BET YAAKOV ATERET TORAH
1750 East 4th Street
Brooklyn, New York 11223

At Mama's Knee

At Mama's Knee

By CHANI GERSTNER
Based On The Memoirs Of Glückel Of Hameln

AT MAMA'S KNEE

FIRST EDITION
First Impression — August 1993

Published by
bp
705 Foster Avenue
Brooklyn, N.Y. 11230
(718) 692-3900

ISBN 0—932351—48-4 (Hardcover Edition)
ISBN 0—932351—49-2 (Paperback Edition)

Printed in the U.S.A.

Contents

DEDICATION

To my father: Without his encouragement, support, and help, this book *could* not have been written.
To my mother: Without her fine example of parenting, this book *would* not have been written.

PREFACE

The 1962 translation of Glückel of Hameln's 17th-century German memoirs unearthed for our contemporary English-speaking world a rare and private glimpse into the somewhat shrouded lives of our European forebears. Better than any history text Glückel provided a portrait of an era most significant and scintillating to the modern Jew. In writing about her family, her community, and her life, she gave us the opportunity to see beyond the centuries — to muse at all the differences the generations have made and to marvel as well at all the similarities.

Glückel began writing her seven-book memoir in Hamburg in 1690, as a sort of therapy after her beloved husband Chaim's death. Therein she instructed her children as she herself had received instruction — through the Torah. The gift she bequeathed to her children was great, for it provided them with a family history rich in tradition and encompassing four generations.

Glückel's descendants cherished and privately preserved copies of the manuscript for two centuries. In 1910, a family member published the memoirs for the first time, in Vienna. This was followed closely by a Hebrew edition published in Tel Aviv. Yiddish and English translations appeared later.

At Mama's Knee is in no way to be taken as another edition of Glückel's memoirs. Rather, it is a novel loosely based on real characters and events that make up Glückel's writings. Thus, for example, Tzipporah, the main character in *At Mama's Knee*, is but a minor one in the original manuscript. Conversations, as well as the order of events, have been fictionalized to accommodate the novel. Great care, however, has been taken to insure that the integrity and validity of the era have been preserved.

Glückel's memoirs have been heralded as an important historical tool, and the purpose of this novel is to present this tool in a more accessible form to young readers.

Glückel died in 1724, yet close to three centuries later,

her message to her children still has meaning to thousands of grateful readers. In her introduction, Glückel includes the following, which, by its simple piety, directness, and honesty, deserves mention here.

The best thing for you, my children, is to serve G-d from your heart, without falsehood or sham, not giving out to people that you are one thing while, G-d forbid, in your heart you are another. Say your prayers with awe and devotion. During the time for prayers do not stand around and talk about other things. While prayers are being offered to the Creator of the world, hold it a great sin to engage another man in talk about an entirely different matter. Shall G-d A-mighty be kept waiting until you have finished your business?

Moreover, put aside a fixed time for the study of the Torah, as best you know how. Then diligently go about your business, since providing your wife and children a decent livelihood is likewise a mitzvah — the command of G-d and the duty of man. We should, I say, put ourselves to great pains for our children, for on this the world is built . . .[1]

1. Lowenthal, Marvin, trans. *The Memoirs of Glückel of Hameln*, p. 2, Schocken Books, New York, 1977.

PROLOGUE

First they bring out the sack of seed pearls, followed by a small pouch of semi-precious stones. Green Moses bids highly for both, and as he walks away from the auctioneer's bench he nods towards Mama. It is his final favor to my father.

I stand to the side, soothing my cranky baby, as the auctioneer barks out the value of the next items. Mama and her seven still unmarried children sit in the back quietly, solemnly watching as each item, precious or impersonal, is brought to the block. I can't sit with them. I can't bring myself to be near Mama as she witnesses the sale of a lifetime of worldly possessions and memories. I feel her degradation, her humiliation.

The dining room set, the goblets, the silver tea ensemble, Papa's collection of *sefarim* . . . each item is accompanied by a story; stories I've heard often at Mama's knee.

There is something that will never be auctioned, I think to myself as I gently rock my child: the stories and lessons I learned firsthand from my mother. They have more value than all the goods auctioned today, and yet they can't feed Mama and her children, or pay the debts my father left behind.

I feel a touch on my elbow. It is my sister Esther. "Look at her," she says, pointing her chin in Mama's direction. "As calm and hopeful as if this were a picnic instead of a desperate turn to support her family."

I nod. "But that is what has always made her special. Her optimism."

Esther agrees. "And it is what she instilled in us. Tzipporah, perhaps she is right. Things do appear to be working out for the best. My father-in-law has a *shidduch* for Mama: Hirz Levy, the philanthropist of Metz."

I smile softly. The proceeds from this sale will more than compensate for the debts and still provide for the family. In a short time, Mama can be expected to remarry. Yes, things *do* work out for the best.

The gavel slams down again and a patron carries off the

barrel of Mama's Passover dishes. My thoughts return to my mother's stories and I realize that they are probably the best legacy I can bequeath to my own offspring.

CHAPTER

Hope And Despair

Sixteen-sixty-two was not a good year for Jews, but that is when I begin my story. I was born that year, a time when every day in a German Jew's life was as uncertain a journey as the next. Outside, the threat of exile, taxes, and soldiers haunted the very gutters of Hamburg, and the everlasting fear of disease and plague hounded our footsteps. Total financial devastation lurked just a few Reichsthalers away, and the shadow of war lay heavy and unrelenting. Inside, however, within our tight, G-d-fearing community, beneath the roof of our small clean ghetto home, we lived a happy life rich with Torah and tradition.

My early memories of Hamburg were joyous ones. I had my younger brother Nathan and my little sister Mata as playmates, and my grandmother near whenever I needed an extra hug or a good story. Certainly mere rumblings of trouble outside did not disturb a healthy, growing child. I know now, though, of the terrible fears that Jewish communities in the Diaspora have always faced, and I have a better understanding of the significance of the two old casks that stoically remain in the front hall of my parents' home.

I remember when those casks first arrived. There was excitement in the synagogue and on the streets that year. People still talk about it. Oh, how we would run joyously to the Sephardic Synagogue every time letters from Smyrna, Turkey, arrived! Oh, what pleasures those letters bore — news of the far away and exotic! The Sephardic youth would appear all decked out in their Sabbath finery, adorned in the broad green silk ribbons of Shabbetai Tzvi. Shabbetai Tzvi! Those were the days we danced in the streets and kissed one another as we heard news of the one we thought would become our King!

I can well understand how easily the Jewish communities rallied around the Imposter. We had suffered so harshly through the tedious birth pangs of the Messiah's coming that we were all-too-ready to believe we were finally witnessing the child of that labor.

Living daily with the rigorous weight of oppression on our shoulders and bearing the lingering consequences of Adam and Chavah's sin on our weary backs, we had nothing but trust and faith in Hashem, and hopeful anticipation for the redemption to see us through another long day. But it is not our place to complain. Instead, we include in all our prayers a passionate cry for the Messiah; so who could fault us for our blind enthusiasm when one finally presented himself?

My father would not accept Shabbetai Tzvi whole-heartedly. His reservations grew when the self-proclaimed Messiah actually married a *sefer Torah*. There was a *chupah* and even *sheva brachos!* Still, though some had their doubts, the overwhelming majority of Jews rallied around the Turkish leader. The reaction from the Jewish world was unprecedented. Whole families — whole communities — sold their houses and lands and packed up in expectation of an early redemption. This was the action my grandparents took. It was a Friday morning when the casks arrived. There was no accompanying letter, just the name "Hameln" inscribed on one of the casks.

Mama was at the market and Papa in the synagogue when the baggage arrived, so the servants just left them in the front hall. All morning Nathan and I played with the closed barrels, alternately sitting on them and daring each other to open one. When Mama rushed in from the street, she raised quite a hullabaloo about their presence in her neat home; but swearing she had much more to do before Shabbos than to waste time investigating their contents, she left them for Papa's inspection. However, Papa too was to disappoint our aroused curiosity.

"Where did they come from?" he asked Bulletproof Jacob, our house-servant.

Bulletproof Jacob just shrugged. "They were here when I came in from the blacksmith. The cook answered the door. She said a messenger came with word of a delivery from the town of Hameln, which was waiting for Chaim Hameln at the Hamburg harbor. I wasn't around to pick it up, so she sent my boy Reuven. I would ask him who dropped them off, only he doesn't speak very much. Well, anyway, that's the story, sir, and seeing as you have them, why not open them?"

My father shook his head slowly. "I can't do that. Since we do not know exactly why they're in our possession, they may not be ours to open. Perhaps we are just safekeeping them for someone. After Shabbos, G-d willing, I will send word to my parents in Hameln. They may solve this mystery for us."

But as fate had it, we learned what was in the casks long before we realized who had sent them. That Shabbos, I was chasing Nathan around the barrels (or was he chasing me? I can't quite recall) when one of them toppled over.

The cover split and out spilled a rush of peas and beans. While the maid packed them back in, we furtively peeked at the rest of the contents and spied dried meats, shredded prunes, and many other types of non-perishable foods. Bulletproof Jacob thumped the other barrel and grandly announced that by the very tone of the echo he could vouch that it was loaded with linens and heavy bolts of expensive cloths. I yanked at his coat and loudly asked if linens clinked, because I had definitely heard something rattle when he thumped at the cork. He blustered on about silver being wrapped in the cloth so that it wouldn't rattle, and that only the very fine ears of the young, and his own, of course, could discern its presence. Then he muttered something about young girls thinking they know everything.

The casks sat in our hallway for three weeks before we received word back from my grandparents. Their response made my mother throw her hands up in despair and caustically ask my father what *we* were to do when the Messiah came for *us*. It seems that in the excitement of Shabbetai Tzvi my grandparents had abandoned their home, their lands, and all their worldly possessions in Hameln and moved to Hildesheim, from where they expected to set sail for the Holy Land at any moment. The casks were to accompany us when we joined them. (My grandfather always insisted that when the Messiah did arrive he would redeem the inhabitants of the town of Hameln before any other in Europe.)

Well, the kegs lay unopened, though somewhat battered by the heavy traffic in the front hallway, for over a year.

Only after my mother insisted that the stench of rotting meat would invade her sleep did we despoil the casks. But we soon replenished them, and kept doing so for close to three years.

I doubt I can accurately describe the disappointment and heartache we Jews suffered at Shabbetai Tzvi's betrayal. We were left frustrated and abandoned by his traitorous and cowardly conversion to Islam. So devastated were some of our weaker constituents that they blindly followed the Imposter down the path of assimilation. Our community, like others in Germany and throughout the world, still bears the bitter scars of his betrayal.

My grandparents returned dejectedly to their house in Hameln, but could not bear any mention of the casks, symbols of their wasted hope. My mother was all for distributing their contents to the poor and tossing the useless barrels into the river for "any foolish fish on the way to the Holy Land." It was my father who insisted that we empty the casks but leave them right where they were as a reminder to us.

"We were not worthy of the Messiah today," he said, "but we will be tomorrow and that is something we cannot afford to forget."

In our blighted community, darkened with disillusion, my father was a glimmering ray of light. It did not take long for my mother to share his spark of brilliancy, and she ended all future street talk of Shabbetai Tzvi with an illuminating "This, too, is for the best."

CHAPTER

The Plague

I was always Mama's special little girl. You may say it is because I am the oldest of her fourteen children, but I believe it is due to the many instances when I was lost to her, only to be brought home again. Even as an infant, I caused my mother to fight like a tiger to retain her little Tzipporahla in her safe arms.

Mama laughs now every time I beg her to retell what she calls the "King Solomon Story." You see, Mama was only fifteen years old when she brought me into her little world of Hamburg, Germany. Beside her in the sickroom lay her own mother and *her* new daughter. Oh, the droves of people that came to visit the mother and daughter both brought to childbed in the same week! As for me, I was swaddled and placed beside my newborn aunt in the small nursery, with an old nurse standing guard.

The trouble began one night when my mother, too restless to sleep, quietly padded into the nursery. Imagine her horror to find the nurse dozing and my cradle empty! Her shrieking awoke the old woman, who emphatically denied falling asleep or any knowledge of the missing baby. Her frantic mutterings of spirits and demons unnerved my poor mother so deeply that she ran screaming down the hall to Grandmother's room. At the threshold she stopped short, for there I was in my grandmother's arms.

"Oh, Mama," my mother giggled. "I feel so foolish! Thank you for taking care of Tzipporahla for me." She moved forward as if to snatch the child.

My grandmother grasped me tightly to her chest. "Glückela, this is my baby!" She turned to the nurse accusingly. "What have you done with my Glückelchen's baby?"

But the terrified woman remained mute, and my mother turned desperately to Grandmother. "Mama, it's Tzipporahla! I can tell!"

That fired a loud argument between Mother and Daughter, which sent the dazed nurse running from the room, shouting something about "King Solomon" and "Fetch me a sword!"

About this time, the commotion awoke my saintly father, Chaim, who, assessing the situation, calmly suggested we look in the other cradle for the missing child. There lay my beautiful aunt. My mother breathed the words I've heard pass her lips so many times: "Everything works out for the best."

Then my mother cradled me in her arms and vowed never to let anyone take me away from her again. However, that wasn't to be the case.

I had heard many stories of the plague — tragic, heroic — at my mother's knee, yet I was still unprepared for it when it came to our town.

It was soon after my sister Mata was born that the whispers of the dreaded plague swept through Hamburg. I was four years old then, and had just spent Rosh Hashanah in the synagogue for the first time. Many Jews fled to Altona, but my father would not travel before Yom Kippur. After the High Holy Days we packed up and left in the night for Hanover. We stayed in my Uncle Loeb's home, which housed the synagogue as well.

On the first morning of Succos, my mother was dressing me when I yelped in pain and drew my arm away irritably. My mother froze for a moment, then gingerly lifted my arm. There, beside my chest, festered a small blistering sore.

I winced as she touched it tenderly and then felt my

forehead with her lips. I yelped again as she suddenly hugged me to her and blew my hair with her breath. Just as suddenly she released me and called for the maid.

"Sophia! Come quickly! Go upstairs to the synagogue and quietly get my husband. Ask him for the name of that barber he saw yesterday, and find out where he lives. Take the child to him and have the barber lay on a plaster. Tell him it seems that Tzipporahla has the same type of sore for which my husband was just treated."

Sophia was gone for awhile, and when she returned she was accompanied by a skinny, lemon-faced woman.

"Let me see the child!" the woman demanded.

My mother pulled me to her. "Why? Who are you?"

"I am a skilled healer," she answered grandly. "Let me doctor the child and she will be cured in time for dinner."

I didn't want the skinny lady to touch me, but my mother pushed me gently towards her. She had barely passed her cold fingers on me for a moment when she gave a terrible shriek and leaped out the door. In a flash, my mother had Sophia by the arms and was shaking her madly. "Who—is—that—woman?" I had never seen my mother so angry.

"Oh, Missus," Sophia cried, "I am so sorry! She wasn't a healer at all! But your sisters-in-law — it was Yenta and Esther — they stopped me! They wanted to know why I was going to the men's section! I had to tell them. Didn't I *have* to tell them? They're family!"

"Yes, yes!" my mother ground out impatiently. "But

what I want to know is, who is that woman?"

"She's from Poland. Rabbi Loeb hired her to clean. That —that witch was listening. She said that since the child just came from Hamburg she lay under grave suspicion. She said she'd dealt with the plague scores of times. She said she would have a look at the girl and say what it is and what's to be done. She — she threatened . . . she said if His Highness the duke heard what befell in his capitol seat and that we hid it . . . They said it was all right to let her look at the child."

Upstairs we heard screaming and running feet. Over and over the woman shouted, "Away, away! Run for your lives! The pest is in the house! The girl downstairs is infected!"

Prayers were forgotten. Terror-stricken men and women ran wildly from the synagogue. Abruptly I was snatched by some stranger and thrust into the garden. I stood still for a minute, too shocked and angry to cry. At that moment the maid was shoved out too, despite her enraged protestations. She pounded on the door as if her life depended on it. As for me, I was more curious than upset about what was going on.

I saw my mother in the house, rapping at the window. She was crying. I heard her shout, "Look at her! Look at my Tzipporahla! Does that look like a sick child to you? See how she plays in the grass. I tell you, it's just a sore! A harmless sore! The same one my husband had not long ago, and which went away. Just a little salve, that's all she needs. Let me go to her! Oh, please, let me go to my baby! Please!"

I couldn't understand why they would keep my mother from me, or why Sophia looked so distressed. She sank to the grass beside me and handed me a buttered roll she withdrew from her apron pocket.

"You see!" I heard my mother screech from within. "See how nicely she eats! She's healthy, I tell you! I beg you, mercy, let me stay with my child!" She slapped at the glass with open palms, until my father sorrowfully pulled her away. My mother's dear face was replaced by the Polish woman's sour one, peering out at me.

"I would give my neck to prove it," she raved. "That girl is tainted."

It was a hot day, and there was not a tree in the garden for shade. Presently my father stepped out bearing a basket of food and a bundle of clothing. I got up to run to him, but Sophia held me back. He started walking towards us, but was halted by a loud hissing from inside the house. He stopped where he was and laid the packages on the ground.

"Sophia," he called across the garden, "listen to our plan. Dress yourself and Tzipporah in these rags. We will hire a gentile to drive you to nearby Peinholz. Tell the peasants that Hanover is overrun with poor, and that the Jews of Hanover could not shelter you for the holy days. Ask to pass the holy days in the town and mention that the Jews of Hanover offer the villagers money for their trouble.

Tell them that the Jews of Hanover will see to it that you get holiday food and that they are paid."

He looked at me longingly, as if he wanted to say more, but he was summoned back to the house. The maid fetched the package and dressed us. I laughed to see Sophia and myself wearing tatters. It was like a merry game to me. I wasn't sorry to wave goodbye to my parents, although they were crying and their lips moved in prayer. I didn't understand that I might not ever see them again.

We were driven to an ugly village and put up in a bare cottage. Hungry and for want of anything else to do, we walked out to the country and strolled in the fields. I knew that today was supposed to be a holiday, and I was confused at the strange events.

By and by, it occurred to me to miss my family, and I began to wail loudly. Sophia could not stop me. In truth, she started to weep too. This was the sorry state we were in when we spotted a group of men approaching.

It was my father, along with his friend Judah Berlin and our manservant, Bulletproof Jacob. Before sitting down to their own meal they had walked the many miles to bring us our food. Everyone in the community had contributed willingly something from their pot for our feast, and the basket was too heavy for just one man to bear.

I recognized my father before Sophia realized who the men were, and joyously took off in a flash. My father cried out in a hoarse voice, "No, Tzipporah! You have to stay where you are." I stopped short, puzzled at these words and at the strange men holding my father back. By this time Sophia had reached me, and she wrapped her arms about me.

They left the basket on the grass, and had started to walk away when I gave this awful shriek and called them back. My father tried to break free and run to me, and they had to bind him with rope to keep him from me.

"But look at her!" he rasped. "How long must we keep up this folly? It's obvious she's hale and hearty. You be my witnesses to that! You tell them we can bring her home!"

His companions made their sorrowful departure and took my father along. The next day they came without him.

This continued for the remaining days of Succos. Sophia, fed up with my nagging questions, finally told me we were quarantined because I was sick. This puzzled me further. I felt fine. Besides, it was Mata, with her weak heart, who was always ill, not I. Still, I was at the age when I thought all grownups were omniscient, and if they said I was sick, then I must be. I lay down on the cot and wouldn't get up until my father sent for me.

Luckily that time wasn't long in coming. With the food, our daily baskets included plaster and ointment, which Sophia applied on my sore. The troublesome boil had all but disappeared by Simchas Torah, and I was finally reunited with my family.

Oh, how I was pulled and hugged and smothered with attention! I thought I would be eaten alive. Even that sour-faced Polish woman kissed me.

My mother would not relax her grip on me for a minute, as if she thought one of the many strangers who embraced, petted, and snuggled me to the point of suffocation would carry me away, and her cherished child would be lost to her again. I became everyone's little darling, the favorite of the village! Now, when I remember the incident, it is not with too much pain.

CHAPTER

The Pot-Brothers

We remained in Hanover for one more week following my release from quarantine, and then journeyed to Hameln, where we would be safe until we could return home. My mother was unhappy to be away so long from her little nest. We were eager for any news of our town, but letters from Hamburg were few, and when one did arrive we had to suspect it might transmit the plague. It had to be fumigated twice before we could accept it, and then, as quickly as we read it, we had to toss it into the river.

I was playing in the garden one day when a dark shadow cast itself over the grass I was sitting on. Startled, I looked up and found myself staring at a tall, fat, hooded figure. The head was bobbing up and down and mumbling in Polish. I was debating whether I should scream, run for help, or be the little lady and politely invite him to sit down. My father's quick footsteps saved me from a decision.

"Green Moses!" he greeted. I looked up to study the oddly named man. What a silly hood. I was fascinated by the many chins he had. "What are you doing here?" My father lowered his voice. "Don't you know we are forbidden to shelter anyone lately from Hamburg?"

"And a *Shalom aleichem* to you too, Reb Chaim." The stranger grinned. "I am only here as a favor to you."

"*Aleichem shalom*, Reb Green." My father smiled. "Surely I would like to speak to you, but my father would not permit me to invite you in. It is against the duke's law, you understand, and we would be exposing ourselves to great danger. How did you even get into the city?"

"I told them I was a scribe to the bailiff from Hachem," he replied, chuckling. "And besides, Hamburg has really been safe for awhile now. But I respect your wishes. We will remain in the garden. All I really wanted to do was to give you the 300 ounces of seed pearls you left in my safekeeping. I know you have a lot of money tied up in them, and the market is falling. I urge you to return with me to Hamburg and sell them right away."

So that is how my father became one of the earliest to return to our city. My mother did not know what to say first. She teetered between begging my father to stay where she knew there was no danger and joyously reminding him to send for his family as soon as he was assured that their home was once again safe.

It wasn't long before my father sent word that it was safe for us to return to Hamburg. He dispatched our manservant, Bulletproof Jacob, to accompany us. At that time, Bulletproof was waiting in Hanover, where he had secured a post-chaise to convey us home.

My mother must have been unhappy with my father's choice for a traveling companion, because she banged around the house ranting about "sponges" and "guzzlers." I asked her what a guzzler was, but she glared at me and sent me to play with Mata.

I, for one, was glad Bulletproof Jacob was meeting us. He was always a jolly man, and he told me the most amazing things! Like when I asked him how a violin makes music and he answered that the violin doesn't make any noise at all and that it is really the violinist making the sounds, only you can't see his mouth move because he practices hiding it. And that that's why he rests his chin on the base of the instrument. That really fascinated me.

At every wedding after that, I would stand by the band and try to catch the violinist moving his lips. I never did.

Bulletproof Jacob said proudly, "That's because we have the best violin players in all of Germany."

My uncle escorted us to Hanover, and when my mother took one look at the local post-keeper, she sat down on the floor and adamantly refused to leave the city until another chariot was hired.

It was Sunday morning and there wasn't another one available, but we were able to find a different driver; that mollified my mother somewhat. While the post-keeper, a short man named Peterson, loudly instructed the new postilion in his duties, my uncle, answering a silent plea in my mother's eyes, begged, warned, and ordered Jacob to take all possible care of his charges, and of all things, not to get drunk.

Jacob promised with a hand over his heart that he would not touch a drop more than he *actually needed*. Then he swaggered over to the post-keeper, and with hand outstretched said loudly, "Farewell, Pot-brother!" But Peterson grabbed his hand and pulled him to the side, where the two of them fell to whispering conspiratorially.

Not much later, we set off for Hamburg. Mama and Mata sat across from Sophia, Nathan, and myself. I had to fight Nathan for the window seat, which I believed was naturally coming to me, since I was the eldest. Nathan insisted that as the only man in the chaise he had a right to the window.

Our bickering continued until Sophia separated us by sitting in the middle. That left a window seat for each of us, but neither of us enjoyed the hollow victory. I felt ashamed for starting the argument, and would have apologized if Nathan hadn't started whining about how he wanted *my* side of the carriage. That was a needless provocation.

Outside of my window bobbed Jacob's very long, very skinny head. There was plenty of room inside the chaise, but Jacob insisted on keeping his "pot-brother" company. You see, the post-keeper claimed he always accompanied his coach at this stage, so now the two of them kept pace, on foot, with our lumbering chaise. I leaned out the window and started teasing him, but my mother sharply rebuked me for misbehaving and shamed me into having more respect for my fellow man. I was sure she was also referring to my fight with Nathan. But Nathan didn't count as my fellow man; he was just a boy, and my brother at that.

"Bulletproof Jacob," I asked curiously, "why do they call you Bulletproof Jacob?"

"Oh, that." He wagged his head tragically. "That, little one, is a sad story, and one I won't be telling without your mama's say-to."

"Go ahead," my mother agreed, leaning back in her seat and closing her eyes. "It will distract the child from her long journey."

"Well, then," Jacob puffed, warming up to his story, "it all began when your dear father's brother Moses, may he rest in peace, had the misfortune to agree to get married, and . . ."

My mother's eyes flew open. "Without the editorials, Jacob, please."

"Of course," he nodded. "Well, as I was saying, your uncle Moses had the pleasure, nay the *blessing*, of getting married, and I was honored to escort him, and his teacher Reb Moshe, may he rest in peace, to the bride's city. Well, as we were riding near Bremervorde, we were attacked by robbers. There must have been about ten of them!"

"You said five the last time you told the story," Sophia accused.

"And my husband said there were only three," Mama said, smiling.

"Well, so what if there were? It sure seemed like ten! They had guns! And in my eyes, each gun counts for another man!"

"Never mind," my mother interrupted with an airy wave of her hand. "Get on with it. You haven't told how bravely you fought."

"Sure did! I gave as much as I got! Only, like I said, they had guns. And we had all the wedding dowry goods. We were all for giving them what we had, only it wasn't enough. They had to shoot us up too. Moses and Reb Moshe, they were hardly shot, maybe just once or twice. Me, I was riddled with bullets! When they brought a doctor to help us, he took one look at me and shook his head, but the others, he said, would pull through. But like your mama likes to say . . . Ma'am, what is it, again, that you like to say?"

"*Mensch tracht un G-tt lacht,*" my mother murmured. I was familiar with that one. "Man plans, G-d laughs." I always wondered at that.

"Yeah," Jacob continued sadly; he seemed to have run out of steam. "Within two days, those two better men passed on, and me, I pulled through to bother you today. Well, anyway, that's how I came to be called Bulletproof Jacob."

We had just passed the city gate, and my mother stuck her head out the window and asked Jacob to take a seat with us so we could reach our night's destination without delay. The manservant wrinkled his long skinny nose and pursed his lips.

"Nah, I feel like stretching my legs a bit. Come to think of it, my friend here has someone he has to see in Langehagen, and I was thinking of joining him. Tell you what. We can walk it as quickly as you can drive, so what do you say we meet you at the station." He didn't wait for an answer, but strode off purposefully in his pigeon-walk style, with his short, plump "pot-brother" waddling quickly behind him.

The weather changed for the worse. The sky darkened threateningly in the late afternoon, and thunder seemed to be chasing us down the road. I kept looking out to see if Jacob was coming — it broke my heart to imagine he would be caught in a storm—but I couldn't see his skinny head bobbing, no matter how eagerly I stretched my neck out. When the rain came down, my mother made me close the flap on the window. Inside the carriage it was very dark. Outside it was hailing a savage mixture of snow and rain, and pieces of ice struck the cloth top of the chaise. As fast as the drops fell, they froze. The wind tossed and buffeted our little conveyance so fiercely that more than once we threatened to topple over.

With the grace of G-d we managed to reach the customs station, about ten miles from Hanover. My mother paid the stiff duty Jews were taxed whenever they entered or left a city, and then urged the driver to make haste, so that we could settle in our inn at a decent hour. The postilion shook his head and crossed his arms over his whip. "Peterson told me to wait here until Jacob comes, and so wait here I do."

We were freezing, and Mata was coughing and wailing uncontrollably. My mother begged the postilion to go, but he was adamant. "No, ma'am. If I do, Peterson will break my neck, as sure as it's raining, and I won't see a cent of pay."

What could we do? Jacob was bound to be along shortly, so we waited.

Those two intolerable hours we spent sitting in the cramped, drafty stationary carriage, with no dinner on hand, in the midst of the most violent storm the area had seen all season, seemed more like two years.

Finally, out of the goodness of his heart, the customs collector took pity on the "wee children" and allowed us into his cozy little room, where it was warm and dry. After about an hour, the collector's nerves were so frayed by Mata's incessant wailing and Nathan's continuous questions in such small quarters that he escaped, or rather stormed out, into the harsh elements. From the window we saw him, arms flailing in the wind, arguing with the stubborn postilion, who was still perched atop the carriage. I don't know what the collector said, but he soon returned with a triumphant grin, and we were off to the inn.

It was a delightful hostelry, small but snug, and we received a wonderful welcome. Most inns were the center of humanity, a hubbub of activity for people from all walks of life. But only in the quaint inns sprinkled about the countryside could you find representatives from the smallest of towns — nestled in myriad unfamiliar nooks and crannies of Germany—sharing a table with wealthier, worldlier citizens of the big cities.

The room was overcrowded with drivers and travelers, yet everyone behaved kindly and oohed and aahed over us soaked children. The innkeeper rushed over with food and provided an excellent beer.

A gabby woman sitting next to me raised her glass and said to my mother, "The beer is from Langehagen, the village with the best Broyhan beer in all of Germany."

At the mention of Langehagen, my mother's ears turned red and she muttered fiercely, "Pot-brothers, eh?"

We sat up late, expecting the two men to arrive, but by the time the babble of both familiar and garbled tongues had petered into a mutual chorus of snoring and the heavy breathing of slumber, the vagabonds still hadn't shown their faces. Resignedly my mother had a bed of straw made for us. I fell asleep the moment I stretched out, but I knew my mother lay awake, listening for the door.

About midnight, I was awakened by a fearful uproar in the room. The keeper of the post burst into the hostel in a drunken fury, and with a drawn dagger attacked the postilion. Our host came running in and pacified the befuddled madman with a little food and drink. When his fury had abated somewhat, my mother anxiously asked him where he had left our manservant.

"Where *should* I have left him?" Herr Peterson growled. "The sot can't hold his drink. He fell down under a hedge somewhere near a pool of water."

This frightened me, and my mother too. For all his misdeeds, Bulletproof Jacob was still a Jew, and he needed help. She begged our host to send two men to search after Jacob and bring him here. No one wanted to brave the storm, and I know it cost my mother six thalers just to rustle up peasants willing to go.

A good half hour from the village they found our good Jacob lying like a dead man, soiled from travel and drink, his good coat and money gone. As angry as my mother was — and she was mightily angry — I could tell she was as glad as I that he had been found alive. She fetched him something to eat, all the while bitingly commenting on how her fine servant, who was sent to serve her, she now had to serve.

When day broke, Bulletproof Jacob was miserable—far too miserable to travel. I kept staring at him, sure that at any moment his long white face would crumple up and cry. By mid-afternoon, my mother's sympathy was exhausted and she insisted we leave. He loaded us up into the carriage, his movements slow and jerky. My mother told Jacob he should seat himself too and not carry on as before.

With one hand over his heart, he said earnestly, "Never again, ma'am. I learned my lesson. Let me just check once more around the room to see if we overlooked anything."

I sat facing the inn door he pigeon-walked into, waiting for him to reappear. After awhile, my mother got restless and she sent in the post-boy to fetch him. When the post-boy had disappeared into the recesses of the inn for quite some time and there seemed to be no signs of his return, my mother climbed down from the chaise and tramped off to the tavern. In no time at all she reemerged with Jacob, roaring drunk, an inebriated post-boy marching tipsily before her.

By now I had figured out what "pot-brother" and "guzzler" meant, as well as "soaker," "souse," "sot," and the few other choice names my mother called the penitent Jacob all the way to Hamburg. I also learned I never wanted to be called one.

CHAPTER

Losing Mata

My father once told me that in the Talmud it is written, "Who prays for what is past prays in vain." Though I loved my childhood years, I wouldn't wish them back, but, oh! how I miss my little Mata!

Though I was never told as I child, I always sensed that Mata was ill. Perhaps it was because I was never permitted to play with her as I did with other children. Or maybe I got the idea from the special attention showered on the bedridden child. I'm not quite sure how I knew.

I never questioned anyone about Mata's health; I just took it for granted, with a sweet childish faith, that the situation would remain the same. Certainly I did not imagine it would worsen.

I do not remember exactly when I first noticed the change of events. I think it was the unnatural stiffness in my mother's back and the grim set of her mouth that warned me. Papa stayed home more than usual and my grandparents came in for a visit even though it wasn't a holiday.

It was my grandmother who suggested to my mother that she tell me stories of my great-grandmother Mata, little Mata's namesake. I didn't think there was a story left that I hadn't already heard at my mother's knee, but I loved hearing them repeatedly, so I sat in the parlor and looked at her beseechingly. The tense expression on her face softened and, turning her youngest child, Joseph, over her lap, she began speaking.

I never met my great-grandmother Mata, but my mother is so filled with wondrous tales about her that she seems to be more an angel than a woman to me. I used to fancy that she had light pouring from her face. Naturally I pictured that face looking a lot like my mother's.

When my mother was just a young girl, the Jews of Vilna were forced to leave the city. Many of the exiles found their way to Hamburg, and my saintly grandfather opened his house to them. Unfortunately, along with their troubles some of these refugees brought the plague with them. Some recovered and some died. My aunt Elkele and my mother took sick as well. Neither fear of contagion nor my grandparents' disapproval could prevent Mata from climbing to the upper garret three or four times a day to nurse the sick and to see that they lacked for nothing.

My great-grandmother did not discriminate in her care, and she tended the Polish strangers with as much diligence as she did her own grandchildren. She was a woman of seventy-four, but moved like one of forty.

She was human, though, not an angel, and tragically susceptible to the disease. As she lay on her deathbed, to her children's amazement she produced a hefty sack. Apparently my grandparents had been giving her a small allowance every week during the seventeen years she had lived in their house. My clever great-grandmother invested those marks rather than spending them. Now she presented my grandfather with over 200 Reichsthalers and these words:

"My son, you have given me more than food and clothing and a place in your home. You have shown me honor and respect, as if I were your own mother. Here is all I have to leave you in return. You deserve it well...but if you were willing to turn it over to my poor, orphaned grandchildren — my Mordechai's two boys. But I leave it to you to spend at your pleasure."

My grandfather's answer was pure gold. "Peace, my mother-in-law. I will gladly forgo your treasure and distribute the money as you see fit. And if G-d is willing, I will add a hundred Reichsthalers of my own."

We all fell silent when my mother finished her story. Our shared wish that our Mata would one day grow into the charitable and righteous woman my great-grandmother had been filled the room unspoken.

Sweet little Mata! She was only three years old when the cycle of her precious life was completed. My parents fell sick from grief, and it was up to me to comfort Nathan, who didn't fully understand the tragedy that had occurred.

Thirty days after dear Mata's funeral, my father called the family together in the sitting room and announced, "All of us have suffered a bitter loss, but grief and mourning harm the body and weaken the soul, and no one depressed in mind can worship G-d the way that he should."

Miraculously we all pulled together following that, except for my mother, who very soon afterwards delivered a beautiful baby girl whom we named Hannah. While Hannah was still swaddled in diapers, a fine baby brother came along to keep her company. At his circumcision we gave him the name Mordechai.

The years of my childhood were both difficult and blessed. I passed my days in a whirlwind of learning and playing. Mata's death was the first personal tragedy I remember experiencing. It was enough for one lifetime, but unfortunately I would meet others along the path of my years.

Always I was conscious of the threat the gentile world

posed to our little people. Many times, when walking with my father, we would pass some Christian on the street, and it made no difference whether he was haughty or a peasant, a young boy or a stumbling old man, the gentile would disdainfully cry out, "*Mach Mores, Jud!*" (Where are your manners, Jew!), and off went my father's hat as he would bow in humble salutation. How I hated to hear that refrain. Almost as much as I hated hearing the gatekeeper call out, "The ghetto is closed! All Jews must be restrained to their houses until morning!" But my mother would optimistically point out that the same gates that locked us in kept the drunken peasants out.

CHAPTER

Aunt Freyde

We suffered another great loss years later. My Aunt Freyde, who was actually my mother's stepsister, passed away. Almost two months to the day from the morning of Freyde's death, my mother appeared at the breakfast table visibly shaken. My father was trying not to smile.

Apparently, the night before Aunt Freyde had appeared to my mother in a dream, claiming that her shrouds had been stolen from off her buried body. I was inclined to believe the dream, and was all for rushing to supply poor deceased Aunt Freyde with another shroud, but my father said that digging up graves is a serious sin.

The next night my mother had the dream again, and my father said to wait and see if the dream recurred on Friday night. Friday night dreams, he told me, are destined to come true. If the same vision visited my mother, then he would speak to the rabbi of the town and fully investigate the situation.

Well, my mother awoke Shabbos morning with a triumphant grin on her face, and first thing on Sunday my father assembled a meeting with the rabbi and the elders of the town. Later that same day, poor Aunt Freyde's grave was overturned, and sure enough, her shroud had been stolen.

We were all surprised — except for my mother and me. Immediately the womenfolk assembled in our house to sew together another shroud.

I had just turned eleven years old at the time, and was therefore permitted to remain in the room. My, the gossiping that went on! The only other women groups that I was permitted to sit in on had no gossip at all. On Shabbos afternoons, mothers and daughters would gather for a recitation and discussion of the week's Torah portion. We were all familiar with the parables and morals of every portion from our own reading of the *Tzenah U'Re'enah*, the indispensable Yiddish companion of every pious Jewish woman for the past fifty years, and the most well-worn book in every Jewish home. But we went anyway.

Bulletproof Jacob kept interrupting the babble with trays of tea and plates of rugelach and a honey-and-nut candy called neunt. When he wasn't serving, he stood outside the room, with his bony head inclined at an odd angle against the crack in the door so he could hear the latest gossip.

The hall light from behind the servant cast the shadow of his skinny head against the wall opposite the window where the women worked, alerting them to the curious eavesdropper. When their voices dropped to foil his intentions, one bony finger extended through the door and pointed at me. When my attention was arrested, the finger crooked. Thus beckoned, I left the room to speak with the manservant.

Plying me with a honey-dripping smile and the pirated sweets which my mother worried would spoil my teeth, he asked me, his longtime accomplice, if the ladies were saying anything interesting. Still swelling from the pride of actually being allowed to sit with the adults, I accepted the candy and bestowed a honeyed smile of my own, but turned smartly on my heels and reentered the room without divulging any secrets.

The women looked up when I returned to my seat. I was made uncomfortably aware of a careful scrutiny of my person. I caught the eye of Baila Krausberger, who leaned over and whispered in her neighbor's ear. Now it was that woman's turn to regard me coolly. Nodding, she spoke up.

"Yes, Baila, you're right. Glückel, isn't it time your daughter settled down already with a husband? She must be now, what . . . twelve?"

My mother turned white and then purple as she swiftly stated, "Eleven." Turning her brightly lit eyes towards me, she quickly mumbled, "Oh, good, Tzipporahla. I'm glad you're still here. You might find this next story interesting. It concerns your dear Aunt Freyde."

I settled back in my chair, glowing with the importance of being singled out and puzzled as to what story there was that I hadn't already heard two or three times at my mother's knee.

"Your Aunt Freyde," she began with a nod towards me, "knew her French like water, and that was to benefit your grandfather greatly. One day, when Freyde must have been, oh, seven or eight, Zeide called her into the sitting room. When she walked in, it was to find three very distinguished gentiles in the room. Her father asked her to sit at the clavichord and entertain the gentlemen. Not only was your Aunt Freyde a beautiful and obedient child, but she was a skilled and talented musician as well.

"As she played, she sang, bless her, Hebrew songs, because that was all she had learned. She played softly, because the men were talking and she didn't want to disturb them. I think she also wanted to know what was going on."

At this point, there was a moment's pause, while all the

women glared darkly at the shadow on the wall. The shadowed head jerked and disappeared for a few minutes, but it was to return before the story was done.

"Apparently, Zeide had loaned one of the noblemen a vast sum, 500 Reichsthalers, I believe, against a pledge. The nobleman had now returned with two of his friends to redeem the pledge. My father excused himself and went upstairs to locate the document.

"Well, while he was gone the men fell into a discussion in French. They planned to take the pledge and slip out without ever repaying the money or the interest. Brave Aunt Freyde kept on playing and singing without even a flicker of an eyelash to expose her knowledge of French. As my father's footsteps were heard returning down the stairs, she changed the words of the song she was singing, and blurted out in Hebrew, 'Oh, not the pledge, my soul, not the pledge — here today, gone tomorrow!'

"Poor dear! That was the best she could improvise in her agitation. But my father was a very discerning man, and he stopped himself short. Very politely he asked the nobleman for his money. Just as politely the nobleman requested his pledge. But my father said firmly, 'First the money, then the pledge.' This went on for quite awhile, as you can well imagine, until finally the customer spun around and cried out to his companions in French, 'We've been foiled! Our game is up! The wench, it seems, knows French.' And hurling threats behind them, they ran from the house as fast as they could."

"I am sure your father was proud of your Aunt Freyde," one of the women exclaimed. "Nevertheless, 500 Reichsthalers is a great loss for your family to have suffered."

"What loss?" My mother laughed. "The very next day, the nobleman returned—this time without his companions—and repaid the loan with due interest. He told my father, 'That was money well spent in teaching your daughter French.'"

At that moment we heard a scream and the crash of broken glass. Sophia was standing at the doorway, the remains of a broken teapot at her feet, her face ashen. We stopped in our project to rush and help her, but she rasped, "Don't stop! Don't stop! Hurry up and finish! Can't you see that *she* is sitting among you?"

We looked around at each other blankly. I felt little bumps rise up my arm and down my spine. Catching Sophia's eye, I mouthed wordlessly, "*Freyde*?"

"Yes! Don't you see her? Oh, just hurry! Please hurry!" Sophia begged, and she ran crying from the room.

The women returned to their task, sewing furiously. All jocularity was ended. The only words now spoken were regarding cloth or thread, and even those were said in a hushed voice. Bored, I left the room.

When I returned, it was to witness the completion of the shroud. Aunt Freyde was dressed and laid to rest. And she was never seen again.

CHAPTER

Journey To Amsterdam

Whenever my father would leave town on business, our house seemed to lose some of its security and spontaneous gaiety. My brother Nathan and I would often be found wandering inside the house or outside in the yard looking for sources of amusement. When my father was home, he would spend his spare time enclosed in a room learning Torah with Nathan. I would be drafted to take care of my younger siblings Hannah,

Mordechai, and Esther. The days when my father was away I was let free to occupy Nathan's time and make sure he didn't get into trouble.

The summer before my twelfth birthday began with my father sailing off to Amsterdam, as he did annually. One morning found me combing the house for Nathan, who had slyly slipped away from my charge.

In a burst of inspiration I tripped into the garden, but halted sharply at the sight of two laborers gesturing wildly and pulling at Bulletproof Jacob. As I tiptoed behind them, I saw the two men fill Bulletproof's palm with coins, and heard him say, "Well, I'll raise your twenty Reichsthalers to thirty. The match will go through. I've got a feeling about it."

"What match?" I asked, completely disregarding my manners and retiring from my position as eavesdropper.

"The match Reb Chaim is making with Elias Cleve," Bulletproof Jacob responded without turning around. "I say the young lady will be betrothed before the leaves turn brown. And I have it on good authority that — what? Hey, Sam. Why are you twitching and winking and . . ."

Bulletproof Jacob froze, then after a moment whirled around. His face paled visibly when he saw me. "Oh, g-good morning, young lady. Just taking some air. Don't you pay us any mind."

"Were you taking bets?" I accused. "Did no one tell you that's a sin? I won't tell Mama if you tell me what match you were talking about."

"Match?" Bulletproof Jacob stared wildly around the garden, then shrugged his shoulders innocently. "Did you hear *match*? I'm sure I meant *latch*. Yeah, these fine gentlemen are going to help me with the latch on the stable. That must be it. Hey, isn't that Nathan I see over there sneaking behind the porch?"

I looked at him strangely, and would have asked some more questions, but he looked so pathetically uncomfortable that I didn't have the heart. Besides, now that I'd found Nathan again, I didn't want to lose him.

I forgot all about the strange exchange I had heard in the garden until one night, later on that week, when my mother called me into her room. In her trembling hand she was holding a letter from my father, and with her other arm she pulled me close and held me against her.

"Do you know who Elias Cleve is?" she asked, her mouth muffled by my hair.

"I know that he's a very important man," I answered, "and that Papa stays in his house when he's in Amsterdam."

"Yes, yes," my mother breathed. "He does. And Elias Cleve *is* an important man. He is a great prince in Israel."

She pulled away from me and stared into my face excitedly. "Do you know that he is a close business adviser and banker to the Dutch royal house and government?! Can you imagine? He is a strict G-d-fearing man who won't compromise his principles no matter whom he is speaking to. Truly we can all learn something from his fear of G-d and his modesty."

I stared at my mother blankly. I saw no connection between myself and this great man of Israel.

"Tzipporahla," my mother said gently, "you know, I was betrothed to your Papa when I was your age."

I felt as if a brick had just crushed my chest. All of a sudden it occurred to me what everyone had been hinting at for the last few days. I was to be married! For a moment a thrill of delight ran through me, but all too quickly it was replaced with a dreadful feeling. I gave a horrified gasp. "Oh, Mama! But he must be ages and ages older than I am!"

My mother looked confused, but then her face cleared and she burst out laughing. Usually just hearing the tinkle of her laugh would be enough to send me giggling, but this time my heart was beating too fiercely, and all I could hear was the blood rushing to my ears.

"Oh, Tzipporahla," my mother gasped, wiping at her eyes. "You can't marry Elias Cleve! His wife won't let you! But" — her face sobered and she gripped my arms — "he has a son. His name is Kossman. They say he's a wonderful scholar. He sits all day learning beside the Rabbi of Cleves. I believe he intends to open a printing business or a publishing house when he marries. Whatever. His wife will be secure."

His wife! Scores of questions pressed my brain. How old was he? Where would we live? What did he look like? Was he shy? Quiet? Kind?

But when I opened my mouth to ask these questions, all that came out was: "I don't want to leave you!"

"Oh, my sweet child!" My mother hugged me closely. "I felt the same way until I met your father. You're a young lady now. Besides, you won't be going far. I took care to make sure you won't be living in Holland — at least not in the beginning. Why, you may settle only houses away from us! What do I always tell you, Tzipporah? Remember, everything is for the best."

"I know." I smiled weakly, but my mouth felt dry as I ran from the room.

Just a few short months later, I was standing on the deck of a small ship that rocked as it crossed the stormy Dollart. I had never been out of Germany before, and Amsterdam seemed worlds away. Nathan had rooted himself in the ship's engine room, and my parents were caring for Hannah and Mordechai, who weren't handling the rolling motion of the sea too well. Queasy from the heaving waves myself, I wondered if my wedded life would be as stormy and unpleasant as my wedding journey. Deeply inhaling the fresh air to quiet my unsettled stomach, I found myself alone with the endless sea and battering wind.

I don't know how long I stood there, but by the time my mother approached me I was deeply chilled. The green hue on her face and the tight grip she had on the railing told me that she too was feeling seasick. I was all for returning to our staterooms and resting, but Mama wanted to remain outside, talking to me.

I guess she must have known what was on my mind all this time because she started talking about her journey to meet and marry Papa. "You know, in the Jewish sector of Hamburg, where I grew up, coaches were plentiful. So when my father-in-law-to-be made the travel arrangements for the bridal party to journey to Hameln, my mother and I . . . I guess we were expecting nothing less than carriages. But you see, Hameln is much more rural than Hamburg. Were we surprised to find open peasant carts waiting for us at the station in Hanover! My mother was so angry that I was afraid she would break the match. But instead, my father started laughing and comically plunked himself down on the floor of the cart, until we were all laughing with him.

"Well, the night we reached your Papa's house there was a great feast. My father-in-law must have sensed my mother's resentment, because he stood up and told the story of when he had traveled to meet *his* bride. You see, since he was bringing 1,500 Reichsthalers with him, he hired a well-known porter named Fish to accompany him. Meanwhile, the bride sent a servant to scout for her groom, and when he came back to her, he cried, 'Do you know how your bridegroom travels? With Fish!' Then my father-in-law turned to my mother and said, "But now, madam, since I have gone from traveling with a fish to traveling with a horse and cart, don't be impatient. There's hope for me yet!' "

I giggled and right away the tension slipped from me. I hadn't realized how anxious I had been during the conversation. All of a sudden warm feelings of excitement stimulated my mind. I *wanted* to meet and marry Kossman.

By then my mother's face had turned even greener, so I quickly escorted her to her bed, where she remained perfectly still until we touched land. In time she was joined by an even greener-colored Nathan, who moaned and twisted as the ship rocked. When the ship passed over particularly turbulent waters, I would visit the sickroom just to hear Nathan gasp and confess all of his sins. I didn't believe for a minute that he was dying, so I found it all very amusing. That was until Nathan cried, "I am at death's door, and my own sister laughs!" Then I sobered, because I didn't want to make him feel worse than he already did.

As soon as we walked onto the crackling green ground of Holland, my attention was arrested by a young man standing beside a carriage near an even younger man. The older one had a flowing dark beard, and he stood impressively erect. I thought he looked kind, and I was immediately relieved. The younger man at his side hurried towards us.

"Let me help you with your bags. I do hope your journey was comfortable." He escorted us to the carriage, and I blushed when I thought that in the next moment I would be introduced to my husband-to-be.

"This is my eldest brother." The boy waved his hand towards the man. "His wife Sarah has prepared accommodations for you in their fine home. I do hope you'll be comfortable."

Wife? I felt confused and distraught, and then the

younger man smiled shyly and said, "I know I'm supposed to wait to be introduced, but I wanted to meet you as soon as possible. You must be Tzipporah. Tzipporah, my name is Kossman."

I looked at the boy and the sparse, budding beard on his smooth chin, and tried not to show my disappointment. I managed a weak smile, and then bent my face into my collar. I had envisioned marrying someone like my father, but now I wondered if I would ever come to respect and love this young boy as Mama loved and respected Papa.

Elias Cleve's house was truly a palace, magnificent enough for kings. All day, elegant nobles and their distinguished ladies came to peep at me and bestow lavish gifts. Prince Frederick—who was next in line to the throne —Prince Maurice of Nassau, and other titled personages came to Cleves to watch our nuptials.

I was stunned, and I know my mother walked around in a daze. Naturally Elias Cleve prepared fitting accommodations for such notable guests. He entertained them with a collation of various sweetmeats and fine wines and fruits, along with a troupe of delightful masked performers who bowed prettily and played all types of entertaining pranks.

You can imagine the bustle and excitement felt by all, and I too thrilled at the celebrations. Yet whenever I thought of my husband-to-be, I couldn't control a sharp stab of disappointment from piercing my heart. We hadn't seen each other since our first meeting, and my image of

Kossman continued to be that of a foolish young boy.

All the plans seemed to go off without a hitch until it was time for the *chupah*. Unless, of course, you count the instance when Mordechai was nowhere to be found and no one recalled seeing him. My mother flew into a panic until he was spotted walking hand in hand with Prince Frederick. The prince would not allow the child to leave his side until the conclusion of all the festivities.

As Kossman and I were standing under the wedding canopy, it was discovered that, in all the confusion, no one had remembered to have the marriage contract written! Nobility and princes were waiting patiently for the ceremony to continue, and beneath the lace veil I felt the heat of their stares. Embarrassment spread over my face. My father and Elias Cleve were frozen dumb, undecided how to quickly and correctly rectify the situation. My mother looked as if she would cry. I would have joined her, when all of a sudden Kossman, the only one who had remained cool and collected throughout the turmoil, asked the rabbi in a low voice if it weren't permissible for someone to read the set contract from a book. Then he, the groom, would appoint a bondsman to write out a contract immediately after the wedding. The rabbi gave a relieved chuckle and said that yes, it would be permissible.

All around me I heard a collective sigh of relief, and with shining eyes I watched my father pat the blushing Kossman on the back. The ceremony was completed and my cup of happiness was filled to the brim. Ever since, when I look at my husband I see in him a strong man, a learned man, a wise man.

A man who would probably never get seasick.

CHAPTER

The Missing Husband

It wasn't easy beginning married life at twelve years of age. If it weren't for my wonderful neighbors I would have had it much harder, and I thank G-d every day that he sent me a husband who would settle in my hometown. My heart goes out to those young girls who make otherwise excellent matches, but must strike out on their own, in unfamiliar settings.

I had my mother near, but my mother, bless her soul, had her hands full with her twin babies, a son named Loeb and a daughter, Hendele, and I was reluctant to draw on her more than necessary. Fortunately for me, the young wives in my town were steeped in *chessed* and would often stop by to offer their help and valuable advice. I made many close friends in this manner.

Across the road lived my old school friend Rebeccah Deutsch, now Frau Lippman. Her husband, Reb Lippman, is a large merry man, and I would often hear him swinging on the front gate, laughing with my husband. His portly belly would hang over the short picket fence, and I, watching from the front window, would always cringe, waiting for the hinges to give way, with gate and neighbor crashing down on poor thin Kossman.

Rebeccah shares her husband's humor, but none of his rotund shape. She looks frail and skinny, but I've seen what she's like ten minutes before the Sabbath, and my, is she spry! Her inquisitive eyebrows are perpetually slanted upwards in the middle, lending her a constant air of surprise. She is quick to speak, and even quicker to pounce on any new gossip.

Whenever there is tragedy, scandal, or bad news hovering in the air, Rebeccah can always be found in the center of it all, following clues, asking questions, pumping passers-by for information, and listening! Always listening! That's the key to Rebeccah, you see. I know that people disdainfully call her a *yenta*, contemptuously sniff at her penchant for gossip, and scornfully ask her if she has nothing better to do than devote her life to other people's misfortunes. But they don't know her like I do. Oh, Rebeccah listens, but she never *talks*.

You see, when Rebeccah sniffs out a tragedy, she is the first to jump in and lend a hand. When the town is buzzing with talk of a scandal, Rebeccah can be found comforting the one involved. I've known her to leave her warm bed in the middle of the night to nurse a sick child or console an older person. She always knows what to supply those who suffer; be it a food basket, a shoulder, or just her time. And for all that she has her despised detective work to thank. To the town she may be an irrepressible gossip — but to me, Rebeccah is an irreplaceable friend.

I'll never forget the part she played in the Moses murder. She was with me when we first heard of it. It was soon after I had moved into my cozy cottage, down the street from my childhood home. My mother, Rebeccah, and Sarah Metz were helping me mend and hang window dressing in the front of the house. Sarah is another good friend of mine, despite the malicious slander about her. Whenever I see Sarah's sad, pretty face, my heart aches for her.

Less than five years ago, Sarah and her husband, Abraham, had moved to Hamburg, just after their wedding. Only a short time later, her husband mysteriously disappeared.

I was only nine at the time, but I remember waking in the middle of the night to heavy pounding at our door. I heard Sarah's high voice desperately begging my parents to recall if they had seen Abraham that night. She banged on all the doors of the town the same way. It was Rosh Chodesh, she would tell anyone who would listen, so he was wearing his dressy red vest, the one with the silver buttons, which she had made him for *sheva brachos*. Had he spent the night here, perchance?

Some of the women spitefully said that Sarah was a shrewish wife, and that her constant bickering had driven him away. Others whispered that he had left home to live the life of an adventurer. It had even been rumored that he was seen in Damascus, masquerading as the Messiah.

Poor Sarah. Her life was in limbo. As an *agunah*, she could not remarry, for no one was able to substantiate Abraham's death. She was not permitted to grieve for him, either, for that same reason. She had confided in me that all the vicious gossip was unfounded — that Abraham would never willingly have left her, and that she feared something vile had happened to him. Poor Sarah. She hadn't even the company of a child to comfort her.

Her slender, nimble fingers were skilled in needlework, and I appreciated her help that day. As we worked, we chatted, until my mother commented sorrowfully, "You know, Aaron ben Moses has been missing for almost a week. Yesterday his wife Fruma came to me in despair. She is sure something wicked has befallen him."

I shot a quick glance at Sarah, who sadly bent her pretty head, chin tucked tightly under her neck. Rebeccah followed my glance, and she pressed her lips together in silent determination. I would have spoken just then, but there was a knock at the door. It was Reb Lippman, come to speak with my husband, who was not at home. When he saw his wife, his face lit up. "Rebeccah, something has been preying on my mind. Perhaps you can help me." His usual cheerful smile had been replaced with a frown. "A few hours ago, I was approached by a servant-girl; I'm sure you would recognize her — she has a club foot. She asked me if I had six or seven thousand thalers on me, because if I did, her master had valuable gold and jewels in his home which he is trying desperately to sell. I didn't have the money, and I told her so. Soon after, I met up with Samuel Heckscher, who said he was likewise approached a couple of months ago, but he didn't go with the servant-girl. I have a bad feeling about this. I'm afraid that Reb Aaron did have the money and it cost him his life."

Rebeccah struck the side of her head with an open palm. "I know the wench!" she exclaimed excitedly. "She approached me too, a few weeks ago, and asked if my husband had a small sum of money to invest. If so, he was to bring it to her master's home, where he had a tidy collection of valuables. I didn't think anything of it then, but now . . . sure, I know the wench. She works for a respectable tavern-keeper one town over, but he has a son as wicked as the night is black. He's a murderer, and I am sure the soul of Reb Aaron is hanging on his neck!"

Reb Lippman looked thoughtful. "We cannot be certain. And even if it is true, there is nothing to be done. This is Hamburg. We are all just privileged guests in our own ghetto. If we breathe a word of this and it is found to be false, we are endangering our lives and the lives of our Jewish brethren in this city."

But Rebeccah was not content. She would not put her theory to rest. For days afterwards she drove all of us crazy, including her husband, who finally groaned a petition for peace. My mother had told Rebeccah her popular "King of Spain" story, and as a result, Rebeccah would not sleep at night, but instead kept a vigilant watch out her window.

My mother told her the "King of Spain" story the same day we had heard the news of Reb Aaron's disappearance. Resting from the weary labor of hanging the heavy draperies, we women sat around my parlor table, drinking tea. My mother began:

"There was a king of Spain who asked a learned Jew what the Hebrew words *Hinei lo yanum velo yishan, Shomeir Yisrael* mean, to which the Jew correctly informed him, 'He does not sleep nor slumber, the Guardian of Israel.' 'Nay!' the king of Spain argued, 'it means, He does not *let* sleep nor slumber, the Guardian of Israel.' You see, the previous night the king was having difficulty sleeping. Exasperated, he took a walk in the wee hours of the morning. The next day, when slanderers came and accused a Jewish family of murdering a Christian boy, the king said vehemently, 'I was out last night and I know the truth. I saw you cast the murdered child onto the Jew's property.' Had the king been able to sleep that night, as he was accustomed to, it would have cost the lives of all the Jews in the kingdom."

That Friday night found Rebeccah restlessly staring out her window. Her husband had long given up on waiting for her and gone to sleep. A noise awoke me in the middle of the night, so I padded to the kitchen for a drink of tea. From across the street Rebeccah saw a shadowy movement in my house, and thinking there was a problem, knocked on my door. That's how the dawn found us sitting together and drinking tea, tucked cozily on the window seat in my newly draped parlor.

With a sudden gasp and a clawlike grip on my arm, Rebeccah paled and then flushed, all the while staring out the window. I followed her gaze. Walking stealthily down the road was a middle-aged couple, the husband bearing the weight of a large chest on his back.

"That's them!" Rebeccah whispered fiercely. "That's the wicked son and his wife." She rose quickly and grabbed her shawl. "I'll bet he's carrying the body of his victim in the trunk." She rushed for the door.

"Rebeccah! Where are you going?" I squawked.

"I must stop them before they destroy the evidence! One *agunah* in this town is enough." She looked at me impatiently. "Well? Are you joining me?"

I tried to stop her, but she was off and running. I was relieved to see her rush into her own house, probably to awaken her husband. I quietly dressed. If he couldn't convince her to stay at home, I didn't want to miss the excitement.

I found her outside, flying from house to house, awakening the men to accompany her on her chase. Unsuccessful in her attempts to arouse a concerned mob, she hurried to the judge's house. The judge came out to his courtyard to speak with her. She spun her tale, speaking earnestly and quickly and waving her arms wildly. The judge looked annoyed and unconvinced, but he finally agreed to send someone to apprehend the couple and search their belongings.

"But," he warned ominously, "should your story be false, all you own will be forfeit to the accused."

Rebeccah nodded her head vigorously in agreement — though I tried to restrain her — and begged his lordship to hurry before the couple crossed city lines and escaped his jurisdiction. By that time a large group of Jews had assembled, and at their high-pitched buzzing I knew they were distressed. The tavern-keeper belonged to an old-line Hamburg family. Nobility often dined in his establishment. Should the accusations prove to be unfounded, the Jews of the city would be in for hard times.

We moved as one down to the harbor, where the tavern-keeper's son and his wife were apprehended just as they were about to board a ship. They vehemently denied knowing anything of a missing Jew, and hurled ominous threats at the entire Jewish community for the inconvenience this matter was causing them.

The community was alarmed. When the judge's men went to open the chest, I half moved as if to stop them, so anxious was I should it not contain any evidence of murder. My fears were not unfounded. The chest contained only the clothing of the couple.

The crowd dashed madly home, and Rebeccah chased after them, calling out, "Good people! Do not despair! Hashem will help us!"

I ran after her, until she stopped short, shaking in her distress. "How can I go home?" she implored, her thin shoulders stooped forlornly. "My friends, my family . . . oh, we will face bad times ahead. . . . And yet, I am not sorry for what I did. I would do it again if I thought it was a chance to spare a Jewish woman from pain. . . . I was so sure they were guilty. I still am."

Wordlessly I took her hand, and together we walked slowly back to town. Along the way, approaching from the other direction and dragging her club foot behind her, was the very wench who worked at the tavern.

Faster than I could think, Rebeccah flew at the girl, and grasping the frightened servant's arms, began to shout rapidly, "It's no use, you know. We know everything already! We know how you lure your victims to your master. We know everything about the murders! Your master and mistress have already confessed and are sitting in jail now. All we need is your confession, and then we will be content. Come, come. Tell us everything. If you cooperate, your punishment will be light."

Poor Rebeccah. I thought she'd gone mad. And then a miracle occurred. The maid began to talk. "I didn't know they would murder him. Honest! I was just following my orders. Oh, that master, he's a wicked one! He made me bring the rich Jews home. I didn't think he would kill them!"

I was shocked, but Rebeccah just smiled triumphantly, as if she had been expecting this disclosure all along. She calmly bore the blubbering servant-girl to the judge's house, and I accompanied them bemusedly. Once she started speaking the maid would not stop, and we learned of the gruesome way Reb Aaron was slaughtered, and of the threshold beneath which his body was stowed.

The wench stammered before the judge; however, with Rebeccah's help, the story was told. We received permission to exhume a body, but were severely warned that should no such body turn up the judge would not attempt to restrain the insulted mobs.

Messengers were sent to speedily recover the evidence. Rebeccah, the judge, and I followed at a slower pace. Meanwhile, news of the false accusation at the harbor and the maid's subsequent confession spread wildly. A cry went up throughout the city, and a countless number of working men swarmed before the murderer's house. As I passed the mob, I heard one man say to his neighbor, "If the Jews find a body, fine and good, but if they don't, we'll tear them apart from scalp to heel." I shivered.

A shout issued from within the house. Two men came out bearing the hideous remains of twenty-four-year-old Reb Aaron, his *tzitzis* hanging intact. Wicked as they were, even during peaceful times, the throng of workers looking on did not let slip one evil word, but quietly left the area.

The body was placed on a cart to be taken to his hometown, Altona, for burial once the Sabbath was out. Mixed feelings of relief for us and sorrow for the loss Reb Aaron's family had suffered left me standing on the street, an undecided smile on my face. I felt a short tug on my sleeve. Sarah Metz stood beside me, her pretty face lit up hopefully. "My husband was a moneychanger," she whispered. "He passed many nights in that tavern. Will you come with me to tell the story of my plight to the judge?"

I nodded, elated that I would have the chance to help the mournful girl beside me. The judge listened intently to her story, then said, "I won't have all unexplained disappearances pinned on this man. Nevertheless, I'll see what I can find out for you."

An hour or so later, the judge sent word to Sarah that the murderer had confessed to killing Abraham and thrusting his body in a lime pit in the tavern cellar. Soon after, a body was discovered; Sarah gasped hoarsely when she spotted a red vest with silver buttons.

Our community mourned deeply that day, for it was as if we had lost both fine gentlemen at once. I was gratified to see some of the older women, who once whispered behind Sarah's back, now comforting her in her grief, and those who had frowned at Rebeccah now shaking her hand and congratulating her.

Though I mourned the loss of our brethren, I was content in one sense. Someone put her arm around me. I turned and impulsively hugged my mother, saying, "You're right, Mama. Everything works out for the best."

She smiled knowingly. "He does not sleep nor slumber, the Guardian of Israel."

CHAPTER

The Difficult Match

Two Jews were accused of stealing precious gems from a Norwegian burgher. The burgher awoke one dawn to learn that a pair of Jewish lodgers had left his house in the middle of the night. Checking his secret hiding place, he discovered that a precious pouch of jewels was missing, and at once suspected his guests of foul play.

Dashing to the harbor, the burgher was informed that the thieves had sailed for the continent in a small hired boat. Hiring a larger craft with four oarsmen, the burgher caught up with the smaller vessel in no time. The burgher and his men forced the Jews to return to the harbor and had them arrested. Despite the fact that they were stripped bare, no evidence was found anywhere on their bodies or in the boat. Still, the burgher had the Jews prosecuted, and they were tortured until they confessed to stealing the jewels and casting them overboard when they realized they were being pursued.

They were condemned to die on the gallows. One of them accepted the only other option available, and embraced Christianity, thereby saving his life. The other went to his death willingly -- dying a Jew, as he was born.

As you can imagine, the news created quite a furor in our community. The names of the thieves were on everyone's lips, and always accompanied with a curse. The Jew that was hung hailed from our town, and all of a sudden villagers from every sector of life, of every age, remembered him as a child. No one had a kind word for him.

"You could tell he was a thief at a young age. He always took the best chair in cheder."

"A boy full of chutzpah! He passed me on the street once when I was with child and he didn't make way."

"He had no business running around and playing in the synagogue on the Sabbath. He should have been made to sit beside his father as soon as he learned to read!"

"I heard his mother used to let him stay in the women's balcony!"

"She always let him run wild. I used to tell her, 'Mirel, you're giving that boy too much dairy food. It's not good for his constitution.' But she never listened to me."

"The year he was born it snowed in April. I knew then that it meant he would bring disaster to the Jews."

The street talk angered my mother, and she would righteously snap, "The man died consecrating G-d's name. The last hour of his life atoned for his sins and earned him a portion in the World to Come. Surely his soul is in Paradise now, and if you ever want to join him, then refrain from this evil talk immediately!"

Her tirades effectively stemmed the waves of *lashon hara* — at least whenever she was around — and I learned by her example how hateful gossip is, and how commendable it is to speak in defense of a fellow Jew. I tell you this story now because I have had use of this valuable lesson at various times in my unquiet life, and the events of the year following my marriage were no exception.

"The mouth can be holy or profane," my father would repeat regularly. "Words have infinite power. They can curse or bless or destroy a man. If you give your word, you may not retract it. Our rabbis tell us to weigh our words on a balance, and to make a bar and door for our mouth." His eyes would darken solemnly. "Never, G-d forbid, should evil talk pass that bar and door."

My mother was more concerned with what should be said than with what was forbidden. She was accustomed to including a small blessing for anyone she spoke of or with. To Mama, refraining from *lashon hara* was not enough; a pious Jew was required to *defend* a fellow Jew as well.

But there were some gray areas which puzzled both my parents. For example, where does diligence end and *lashon hara* begin when the talk concerns a *shidduch*? How much leeway does one have to investigate the past of a potential son-in-law or daughter-in-law, since the investigation may disclose wrongful behavior?

Shidduch was the most commonly thrown-about word in my parents' home those days. Nathan married two years after my wedding, leaving eight unmarried siblings, including the new arrivals, Samuel and Früdchen. A few years later and with great difficulty my father was able to secure a heavily taxed matrimonial permit, a governmental document designed to stem the growth of the Jewish population. Without one, a Jew cannot marry in Germany. When it is granted, it can only be used by one member of the family, and it is valid for just a year.

With the matrimonial permit in hand — to the envy of our neighbors — my sisters Esther and Hannah blushed whenever a family member teased them. My brother Joseph, though in his teens, was not in a position to consider marriage at the time. When Nathan had married, he settled in Hamburg and, according to another royal law initiated to control the Jewish population, only one son at a time could marry and settle in his hometown. Joseph needed to find a trade and place of residence satisfactory to him before he took a wife.

In the early spring I received word from my father-in-law, the renowned Elias Cleve. He had a *shidduch* to propose for Esther, but he requested that I not mention it to anyone until my father was again in Amsterdam. At that time my father-in-law would have the chance to suggest the match in person. Therefore, no one could understand my excitement when my father's trade took him off to Holland soon after Pesach.

The morning that my mother burst into my cottage excitedly waving a letter in the air, I feigned surprise at the news of Esther's betrothal to a certain Moses Krumbach, the son of the wealthy Abraham Krumbach of Metz. But my resulting happiness was genuine. My mother seemed happy as well, which was why I was confused by her sudden grief just a few days later.

Apparently some anonymous well-wisher had thought it advisable to inform us that the *shidduch* was in every respect a disadvantageous match. Moses, we were warned, had many failings and defects, and to ally our good name with his would be a tragedy. My mother was heartbroken. When my father came home from Amsterdam, he announced that the betrothal had been signed.

My father refused to hear the details of what was said about Moses Krumbach. He told my mother gently, "Glückel, you are Esther's mother. I trust you to act in her best interest. Do whatever you feel is right."

My mother sat down and, working far into the night, carefully constructed a tactful letter to the boy's mother. In it she mentioned what she had heard, along with her personal opinion, which didn't give much credit to *lashon hara*. However, since it was her daughter's life at stake, she was respectfully inviting Moses and his mother over for a short stay so that the family could meet him. She concluded the letter with a brief note stating that, if Moses indeed was as fine a boy as she believed, the wedding would be one such as had never before been seen in Hamburg. However, if, G-d forbid, the boy did indeed have those failings mentioned in the letter, she begged Frau Krumbach to understand, as one mother to another, that the match would have to be broken.

I know my mother agonized over every word, dreading that they might cause pain to Frau Krumbach. But despite Mama's painstaking effort, the responding letter was cold and bitter. Frau Krumbach contemptuously wrote that she had indeed planned a short visit so that our family would get to know her son, but since we'd unforgivably insulted her by paying heed to malicious reports, she had canceled her trip. If my mother chose to travel to Metz, she would be more than welcome in the Krumbach home. Her letter ended with a caustic reminder that a betrothal was signed, and how much was the word of a Hameln to be trusted.

As Frau Krumbach refused to leave Metz and my mother refused to leave Hamburg, the *shidduch* was brought to a standstill. No wedding date was set, and Esther walked around with a mournful expression.

Not long after, my parents received word of another

shidduch possibility, this time for Hannah. The groom was to be the honorable Baer Cohen, a widower far older than my sister, but highly respected in his community. His late wife Bela was a distant cousin of mine. She had died leaving no children of her own, but entrusted in her husband's care her young orphaned niece Glückchen. The match was a fine one, and my parents were considering it favorably.

The morning before my parents were to sign the betrothal, I was awakened early by an incessant knocking at my front door.

It was my neighbor Rebeccah Deutsch. The worried, flushed expression on her face warned me that she was distressed about something. Concerned, I ushered her into the parlor and pressed her to tell me what was on her mind. She was reluctant at first, but then with a grimace she began. "You don't know how I hate to tell you this, Tzipporah. You know I am not a talebearer, and I hate repeating stories I've heard, but I feel I must make an exception in this case."

Thinking that perhaps she had heard fresh news concerning Moses Krumbach which would sway our decision one way or the other, I leaned forward eagerly. What I actually heard shocked and dismayed me.

"Don't let your sister marry Baer Cohen!" Rebeccah began in an agitated rush of words. Her face was flushed. "Only misfortune will come from it. Trust me!"

I was overwhelmed. Though I did trust Rebeccah, I now

told her that I refused to speak out against a *shidduch* when I was unaware of problems, and all reports pointed to Baer Cohen as a wonderful man.

"Oh, he is!" Rebeccah hurriedly stressed. "But he is misled, and I am afraid that he will pay for his mistake."

I shook my head confusedly. "Rebeccah, you are speaking in riddles. You can't mean that Hannah isn't a good enough match for him. You know my sister as well as I do."

She sighed resignedly. "I see I will have to tell you all I know. Baer Cohen cannot marry your sister because he has already given his word that he will marry Glückchen."

"His niece?!" I was incredulous.

"Yes. You see" — Rebeccah twisted uncomfortably in the cushioned seat — "on her deathbed, Bela Cohen made her husband swear that he would marry her niece, and he promised."

I was reluctant to believe this. "Do you believe this is the truth? Or is it just hearsay?"

She blushed. "I was with Bela when she passed away."

There could be no denial of the facts now. My parents were duly informed, and Baer Cohen was approached. Abashed, he admitted that he had indeed promised to marry Glükchen, but he insisted he had been deranged with grief at the time. He begged us to understand that he had raised Glückchen as a daughter and could not bring himself to now marry her. He was prepared to marry Hannah. Nonetheless, my parents were afraid to finalize the match. As my father had often said before, the spoken word has awesome power, and promises should not be made or broken lightly.

Soon after, we received word that Baer Cohen had married a daughter of Tevele Schiff, one of our neighbors. Scarcely a week after *sheva brachos*, the young bride was involved in a fatal riding accident. Almost immediately, though it was the scandal of the town, Baer Cohen took Tevele Schiff's other daughter in marriage. Meanwhile, we were back where we started; three children of marriageable age, no wedding dates, and a hard-won matrimonial permit whose expiration date was ticking nearer, day by day.

The state of poor Esther's *shidduch* remained at a standstill for many months, both mothers adamantly refusing to budge from their respective towns, until, ironically, an act of anti-Semitism reminded my mother of the importance of the spoken word.

One day, soon after Succos, our little town was stunned with news of betrayal. Two baptized Jews, perhaps to garner praise from the Christians or perhaps to validate their conversion, went to the king and accused the Jews of blaspheming in our daily prayers. The prayer they singled out was the concluding song, "Aleinu," and the phrase they dwelt on went, "For they (idol worshipers) prostrate themselves to vanity and nothingness, and pray to a god that cannot deliver." This was a ridiculous accusation, and to his credit the king judiciously investigated it. The gentile theologian he consulted disputed the claim of blasphemy, and the king cleared the Jews of the charge.

My mother said there was a lesson to be learned from this affair. If gentiles recognized the value of the spoken word, she reasoned, how much more so should we? If a gentile king does not accept evil gossip, it behooved us to do the same.

At that moment, Mama made up her mind. "I won't accept *lashon hara*," she announced. "These malicious stories must be investigated. If Moses Krumbach won't come to Hamburg, then I will go to Metz. But investigate the stories I must."

We waited tensely for Mama's return from her investigative trip. The day she returned, her countenance bore no hint as to what had passed, and poor Esther had to remain with bated breath until Papa came home from the synagogue before discovering if she was to be a bride or not.

Mama prefaced her announcement with, "Of course, only time will tell if I've chosen wisely... but... I've met Moses and I've seen nothing that displeases me. In fact, I've been very pleased indeed. The match is on!"

So we used the matrimonial permit in time after all. The wedding celebration was a joyous affair, made all the more gay by the announcement of a favorable match for Hannah. Moses ben Loeb was the honorable name of her future husband, the son of the man who, in 1665, was most instrumental in convincing Prime Minister Oliver Cromwell to readmit Jews to England. Since Moses intended to reside in London after the nuptials, no permit was necessary, and a wedding date was quickly set. Joseph began talking about joining his future brother-in-law in his English trade, and so I felt that his *shidduch* would not be far behind.

During the wedding feast we heard distressing news of Baer Cohen. His third wife had passed away years before her time, and a Jewish court in his town requested Glückchen to absolve him of his promise to marry her. My father's friend Judah Berlin, who was the son-in-law of my Uncle Samuel and a well-known man of means, announced that when she did he would be honored to betroth her to his son.

At the mention of Baer Cohen, I trembled, as I considered that my dear sister might have married him. After all, all three of his wives had died, not a good sign. My mother had a faraway look in her eyes. "There's a lesson to be learned from this, Tzipporahla. Words are not to be trifled with. A broken word has wrought tragedy. Somebody else's evil words almost had the power to break our solemn word. I'm thankful we didn't break our promise to Moses Krumbach."

Mama had cause to be much more thankful when many, many years later she would live out the rest of her days comfortably, as a valued guest in the home of her married daughter, Esther, and Moses Krumbach, her fine, upstanding son-in-law.

CHAPTER

The Comet

The year 1682 (5442-43) will forever remain in the minds of our villagers as the year the star with the tail swept across the sky. For myself, it was a year I mostly spent in bed, waiting for my first child to be born. And for my mother, it was a year of judgment. Allow me to explain in order of events.

We were walking silently to the synagogue on Tishah B'av to hear the reading of Megillas Eichah. We were dressed somberly that July evening, and our cloth slippers slapped the ground softly as we stepped. I felt certain I was pregnant, and thought sadly that my baby was missing its customary dinner.

As we neared the tall wooden building in the center of the town, we heard a shout; before our eyes, scores of Hamburg Jews streamed out of the synagogue and stood gaping in the gutter, pointing to the sky. We followed their gaze and gasped in surprise. Blazing a fiery path through the deep blue summer sky, the glowing head of a comet raced above us, its flaming tail trailing sparks behind it. Children laughed. Women cried. Men swayed together, praying earnestly that no calamity befall them. I felt a stab of apprehension, but my mother's comforting touch reassured me.

"My grandmother once saw a star just like this one," she whispered in my ear. "The gentiles went crazy. They thought it was judgment day, and that the world would come to an end. We Jews, of course, thought it signaled the advent of the Messiah. But" — a shrug, a sigh — "the Messiah didn't come, and the world is still here. So who knows what this sign from heaven means?"

It was late in the evening before our community was able to assemble again to hear the reading of Eichah. This year, the loud weeping of the women overpowered the mournful tone of the *chazzan*. It was a terrible sight to see: daughters clutching their mothers tightly, burying their faces in aprons, instead of following the Megillah.

The comet incident was not forgotten quickly that year.

Whenever there was a hint of trouble—on the street, at the synagogue, in the home—the "blazing star" was mentioned in a horrified whisper.

But life had to go on. The recent weddings plus the new arrivals of Mama and Papa's twelfth and thirteenth children did not do much to alleviate my parents' financial burden.

Business was a hard and dangerous enterprise for my father. His jewelry trade took him on hazardous journeys to strange foreign towns. I remember how Mama suffered mortal agonies whenever my father's trade led him out of our village. I'll never forget the time when Papa went to the Frankfurt Fair with two other merchants. First one, then the other became sick and died. Through spending a great deal of money and by calling in favors, the Jewish community was finally able to recover one body, but the other tragically never received a proper Jewish burial. All goods belonging to a Jew who dies at the fair automatically become forfeit to the prince of Frankfurt, and it was a long time before my mother could tolerate another of my father's business trips abroad.

In the spring of 1682, my father had fallen sick at the Leipzig Fair in Saxony. To be ill at the fair was dangerous for a Jew, for should he, G-d forbid, die in Saxony, all of his possessions were forfeit to the state. Judah Berlin happened to be in Leipzig at the time, and to his everlasting credit he nursed my father back to health and accompanied him home to Hamburg.

Once home safely, at Judah's proposal and my mother's

recommendation, my father and Judah entered into a business partnership. Judah was fearless and ambitious, and eager to travel anywhere on the continent to further my father's trade. Since worry and fright accompanied Mama whenever Papa traveled, she was favorably inclined to the partnership. My father was more cautious. He refused to enter into an agreement unless Judah promised that, if the partnership made less than two thousand thalers a year, my father would be able to dissolve the compact immediately.

My father laid out two thousand thalers to start the business off, but at year's end Judah's trading had earned less than one thousand thalers, certainly not enough to support two households. My father traveled to Judah's home in Hildesheim, and of free will and in friendship he and Judah dissolved the partnership. The business had a small fortune in unsold jewelry which my father turned over to Judah to sell. He was to send us the proceeds.

Months passed and we still hadn't heard from Judah. My father traveled to Hildesheim to find out what was holding up the sale. What he discovered both shocked and angered my family. Judah claimed that the money from the sale belonged to him. He said that, by my father's dissolving the partnership, he, Judah, had been forced to forgo thousands of thalers in future income.

What could my father do? However misled and unjust Judah was, he still held a large sum of our money. The one thing to which Judah would agree was to appear before a *beis din,* a Jewish court, but only if the judge were a rabbi from Hildesheim. My father returned home dejectedly to ask the honorable Reb Ascher to be his arbiter and argue his case for him. By agreeing to try his case in Hildesheim instead of on neutral territory, my father was already at a disadvantage.

The good Reb Ascher accompanied my father to Hildesheim and defended him before the *beis din,* but he could make no progress standing alone against two other arbiters. What was most shocking and upsetting was that the whole Jewish community of Hildesheim joined in to condemn my father. The case seemed close to entering the civil courts, but my father swore up and down that he would give up his entire fortune rather than create a *chillul Hashem* by involving a civil court. As a result, my father had to pay close to a third of his fortune to Judah in accord with the *beis din*'s ruling.

I was unsettled about this outcome for weeks. My father moved on with his business and his life after the unfortunate court reckoning, but I couldn't be consoled. In fact, my father and Judah renewed their friendship, but I couldn't be so forgiving. I felt cheated and disillusioned that an entire community and its rabbi could be so false and dishonest. My father perceived my frustration, and one day he sat me down for a long talk.

"Right or wrong, the decision of a Jewish court must be upheld," he told me sternly. "The Talmud tells us that Shimon ben Shetach executed eighty witches in Ashkelon according to the laws of the Torah. In revenge, the relatives of the witches hired young men to falsely testify that Shimon's son had committed a capital offense. The young man was tried and condemned to die. As he was about to be executed, the witnesses confessed that they had lied, and Shimon ben Shetach nullified the decree against his son. But his son said, 'Father, let the law run its course at the expense of my life.' You see, there is a Jewish law that once a witness has testified he is not permitted to retract his words. According to this law, Shimon's son insisted that he could not be exempt from the ruling of the court." My father shrugged. "What's a third of my fortune in comparison to the life of a *tzaddik*?"

I shook my head stubbornly. "A holy court should have stricter standards."

"There is only one truly holy court, and there is only one true Judge. Men make mistakes. It is not for us to judge. But we must abide by our Sages, who tell us, '*Al tifrosh min hatzibbur*—Do not separate yourself from the community.' You must assume that the rabbi, Judah Berlin, and the townspeople of Hildesheim believed in what they fought for and were not aware of the injustice."

I felt somewhat better after that. My anger dissolved and I hurried over to my mother. I knew that she wasn't harboring anger anymore, but I could tell that she was not at peace, either. Just that morning I had heard her sigh to herself, "*Die ganze Welt ist voll Pein, ein jeder find't das sein* — The world is one long groan, which each man calls his own." I wished to comfort her the way my father had consoled me. I repeated to her the words of my father, the Talmud, and our Sages. With lips drawn in a straight line, my mother mumbled, "Our Sages also say, 'The sword comes upon the world because of the delay and perversion of justice.' "

When some days later my father made a spectacular sale which more than recouped his losses, I heard my mother murmur, "G-d rewards the innocent . . . *and* he punishes the guilty."

That Pesach, both of our families traveled to Hameln to stay with my grandparents. On the way, we stopped off at Hildesheim to spend Shabbos there.

Shabbos morning, Mama, three of my younger sisters, and I mounted the three flights of steps to the women's balcony of the tall wooden synagogue in the center of the town. Barely had we sat down when one of my sisters began to cry plaintively for a bottle. My mother stood up and, grasping the crying child in her hand, led her out to the stairwell. The two other girls, unwilling to stay in a strange synagogue without their mother, scurried after her. I, seating myself carefully, remained with just the company of my unborn child, and settled back comfortably to enjoy the great singing voice of Cantor Jokel of Rzeszow.

What happened next is, to this day, not clear. A loud crashing noise rumbled through the ceiling. Panic and confusion ensued. All of a sudden, someone remembered the comet sighted last summer, and cries of "The world is coming to an end!" and "The sky is falling in!" resounded through the rafters of the synagogue. A mighty fear descended upon the congregation. People scrambled madly for the doors. Each one thought of nothing but saving his or her own life.

There was a crush of women streaming down the stairs, and those that fell were trampled mercilessly beneath the stampede. In a few minutes, more than fifty women lay knitted together on the three flights of stairs, the living and dead glued in one writhing mess. The terror-stricken survivors ran headlong into the street, their hair uncovered, their clothing torn. The menfolk rushed over and wrenched and pried apart the women, each only intent to save his own. This added to the turmoil. When the dust had settled, six young women were dead, while more than thirty others were seriously injured.

Throughout I had remained frozen in my seat. Though prompted to run by the constant stream of women rushing past my bench and by concern for my mother and sisters, whom I had last seen heading for the stairwell, still I could not move. This perhaps saved my life and the life of my baby. Finally Kossman found me, and against my protestations forced me to return to the house where we were staying. When we entered the parlor it was to discover Mama sitting soundly, surrounded by my sisters.

As she sipped a little schnapps, a faint smile passed her lips, and she motioned me beside her. "I have finally been vindicated," she whispered as I gingerly sat in a chair.

"Your mother has a strange story to tell," my father said bemusedly, staring out the window.

"As your sisters and I were going down the steps of the synagogue, all of a sudden — I can't tell you how, but out of nowhere — a pale, veiled woman appeared and wrapped us in her cloak. I was so surprised that I couldn't say anything at first. Then we heard this crashing sound, followed by crowds of women rushing into the stairwell. I could see them bearing down on us. I was so sure we would be trampled to death, but oddly, not a single woman touched us. They were all falling on top of each other, and I could hear awful screaming, but not a single one fell against the cloak that surrounded us. After a short time I heard men pulling their women out, and the screaming stopped. Without a word, the woman disappeared, taking her cloak with her. We walked out of the synagogue, dazed but miraculously unscratched." Mama was still smiling faintly as she closed her eyes and leaned back against her chair. "It's tragic what happened today. Thank G-d there weren't more people hurt. . . . I wonder what that sign from heaven meant."

Mama was vindicated. What no earthly, mortal court was able to achieve, the heavenly tribunal, the omniscient, omnipotent Judge of all creation, had done. Mama was vindicated, and the town of Hildesheim had been punished.

We never did find out what had made that crashing noise.

One week later, my first child, Rachel, was born.

CHAPTER

10

Superstition And Faith

Papa never cowered from his trips out of town, even though danger for a Jew was always imminent. There was the time when Papa and the other Jewish merchants returning from the Winter Fair in Frankfurt failed to arrive on schedule. It was in 1689, and I was pregnant once again. Rebeccah flew to our cottage in a tizzy. She had just heard from the woman who brought the mail that a skiff conveying Jewish and Christian travelers across the River Elbe had been crushed by an ice floe, and that all on board were drowned.

My mother was a flurry of inconsolable activity. Not permitting herself to grieve, she raced off into the storm-ridden night, with young Rebeccah and myself panting heavily in pursuit, ducking our heads to dodge the sheeting rain, attempting to keep pace with her. Halting at the waterfront inn, she banged heavily on the door and demanded that the innkeeper send the man named Green Moses down at once to speak to her. At the sight of the tall broad man sweeping hurriedly into the tavern, I smiled faintly, recalling the hooded figure who had so scared me as a child. Now his bearded face was streaked with gray.

My mother implored Green Moses to take to horse and gallop to the ford at once and discover what had happened. After he rode off, we anxiously plunged once again into the villainous weather and returned home. When we burst into the house, it was to discover that my father had returned and was calmly drying his clothes in front of the fire. Everything that the woman had learned at the post was a lie. Nevertheless, it was a long time before my father could prevail upon my mother to let him journey again.

But life must go on, and with several children yet unmarried, my father had to procure a living. So my mother would fill the time of my father's absence by retelling stories about her faith to her children. Her intentions may have been to comfort *us*, but I could tell her own spirits benefited from the stories as well.

A few weeks before Shavuos, Papa left for the annual

Leipzig Fair. During his absence, Mama made it a custom to stop by my house every afternoon and amuse me for a spell. Due to my pregnancy I wasn't permitted to leave my bed. My friend Rebeccah would visit too, and we would pass the hours chatting pleasantly.

One day, when I was feeling a little better than usual, I sat myself upright beside the open window, inhaling the fresh spring air. I heard wild barking, and peering down the street, I commented idly, "Oh, look. Farmer Schultz is moving his herd of sheep again."

With a small cry Rebeccah shot to her feet, leapt to the window, and swiftly drew the curtains closed. I had to lean back in my chair to avoid being knocked in the eye by one of Frau Lippman's flying elbows.

Breathing heavily, she turned to me and said reproachfully, "You should know better than to look at animals in your condition."

I stared at her, open-mouthed. "Rebeccah, you can't be serious."

"I'm *very* serious," she retorted angrily. "Who knows what kind of a beast you will deliver if you . . ."

I was laughing very hard now, which caused the baby inside me to punch at my stomach painfully. "Oh, Rebeccah," I said, gasping, "that's superstition. What are you going to tell me next—that whatever I crave for I must be fed on the spot?"

"Yes, Tzipporahla." The serious tone of my mother's voice surprised me. "If you have the strong desire to eat anything in your state, please make sure that you get it."

"Mama, what are you saying? You always told me that superstition shows a lack of faith. And the Rambam speaks out so strongly against superstition."

"I'm not asking you to believe in superstition, Tzipporahla. I'm just telling you that a pregnant woman should be given what she craves. You should know, Tzipporah, it's the halachah. Even on Yom Kippur, she must be given a taste of what she craves or it is bad for the mother and the child. Let me tell you a story that happened when you were probably too young to remember.

"When I was pregnant with your brother Joseph — you know he always did give me trouble, that one — my mother asked me to accompany her to the market. It was Kislev, I remember, and one peddler had just come back from the East with a basket full of medlars. I hadn't seen medlars since the summer, and my, those fruits looked good! I decided I would buy some on the way home. But one thing led to another, and we were so busy buying delights for Chanukah that when night fell we rushed home, and I forgot about the medlars. Later that evening I remembered the fruit and was upset with myself, because I truly yearned to taste it. Still, I went to bed in high spirits.

"Sometime in the middle of the night I gave birth. It was a boy, and Papa was so happy his saintly father would be given a name. I was tired, but very happy. Then I noticed that the womenfolk in the house who had come to help me with my labor were whispering conspiratorially, and not one told me *mazel tov*. I became suspicious and demanded that they show me the baby. After much deliberation, they brought the baby to me, along with a lit candle for light. Oh, Tzipporahla. The infant was covered head to toe with blotchy brown spots, and he just lay there, immobile. He wouldn't even open his mouth to eat. As the days passed, he grew feebler.

"On Shabbos, the day before his *bris* should have taken place, I called my mother into the room excitedly. I begged her to send out the Shabbos *goy* to find the peddler with the medlars and bring them to me at once.

"My mother grew irritated at my irrational request. You see, it was storming outside, and no peddler would be around. I explained to her that it suddenly occurred to me that the baby's malady might be due to my not satisfying my craving for medlars when I pined for them. My mother told me it was rubbish, that she had given birth to many healthy children despite denying her cravings. But I insisted, and the German woman was sent out.

"It was a miracle, but she came back shortly bearing a handful of medlars. I grabbed one and squeezed the fruit's pulp gently along the infant's still mouth. You should have heard me scream when the tip of a little pink tongue stuck out and began to lick its lips. I held the pulp against his mouth and he sucked on it so greedily I thought he would swallow it whole. From that moment on, he would allow me to feed him, and the brown spots began to fade. By the next morning he was healthy and well-formed, and we had the *bris.* So your brother was accepted among the Children of Israel at the appointed time, after all."

I shuddered. "Well, then . . . I guess superstition *can* be believed in. But where does that leave faith?"

"I didn't tell you everything." My mother leaned forward, her dark eyes glittering. "I didn't tell you that your father stood in the corner for hours saying Tehillim." She leaned back again. "So, Tzipporahla, keep your faith. It's all a Jew can take with her wherever she may go. Nevertheless, if you should crave something now, eat it."

"And the animals?" Rebeccah asked excitedly.

My mother's eyes twinkled. "Well, we all know from the *Tzenah U'Re'enah* that Yaakov Avinu influenced the birth of lambs by the kind of staff he placed before their mother. But are you comparing my dear Tzipporahla to a sheep?"

We were very merry that afternoon; it would be the next to last time my mother would visit me before the birth of my child.

CHAPTER

An End And A Beginning

I f someone were to ask me why I bother to record my memoirs, and why I insist on interweaving my private reminiscences with preaching, my answer would no doubt puzzle the questioner. The reason is faith.

This book was undertaken as an expression of my faith in Hashem. It is a vehicle for the faith of my people. My upbringing, the events of my life, the people who surround and love me all can be credited with fostering my faith, the faith shared by the Jewish people throughout the ages. I've met those who live day to day without believing, cynically expecting the worst. My heart goes out to these anchorless people, for whom the world must seem to be one dark void.

A Jew living in perilous times — and truly, when do Jews not? — has only his faith in the One Above for his security. Mama has gone a long way in encouraging that faith within each of her children. Even though her courage falters sometimes, I've seen her suppress her fears and loudly proclaim full trust in Hashem, for her children's benefit. Truly there is a lot to worry about; starvation, pogroms, war, disease. One could be overcome with fear. But my father, Chaim, taught me that fear is a sin.

The day after my mother told me her story of the medlars and Baby Joseph, she stopped by, only to worriedly wave a letter at me. Most of the men at the Leipzig Fair had returned that morning, and one of them had delivered the letter.

Green Moses, my father's business companion, wrote the letter, informing us that Papa wasn't feeling well enough to travel, and that he, Green Moses, would stay behind with Papa until he recovered. The letter sounded reassuring, and Papa had signed the bottom. But, oh! what a signature! His hand must have been shaking so badly, for not one mark was clearly discernible, or recognizable as his handwriting. Instead of reassuring us, the letter made us uneasy.

You can imagine our anguish, but my mother saw to it that we never lost our faith, and indeed, a few weeks later Papa returned home. He looked dreadfully ill, and Mama called for a doctor immediately.

I left my house to visit Papa. He was happy to see me, but he was concerned to see me walking around in my late stage of pregnancy. For my part, his appearance caused me distress, for a deathly pallor hung over his thinned face. It broke my heart to see him this way. I sat with him until Dr. Abraham Lopez entered and motioned me to leave.

Mama found me in the front room. My despair must have shown on my face, for Mama sat beside me, quietly holding my hand.

"You know, the doctor wasn't always religious. His story is an interesting one."

I looked at her in shock and with a little anger. Here was Papa, his health dwindling rapidly, and instead of comforting each other, Mama was gossiping. Mama, who had always preached against gossip.

If she sensed how I felt, she ignored it. "Have you heard of Queen Elizabeth?"

I nodded. "She was Queen of England during Grandmother's time."

"Yes. There were no Jews in England then. There hadn't been any since 1292, when King Edward the First expelled them. But apostates were allowed in. One such man was Elizabeth's private physician, Richard Lopez, who was born in Spain into an assimilated Jewish family. He learned medicine in England, where he became the official royal physician. He was quite favored by the queen, which made him unpopular with the members of her court. Somehow, I don't know why, he was accused of attempting to poison the queen, and was subsequently hanged. It was never proven, but the hatred of Jews, even those who had converted, ran so deep in England that he was convicted almost immediately.

"How do you think the news affected his family? Well, some of those who were already assimilated decided to convert. The others refused to belong to a race that would kill an innocent man. On the other hand, they would not serve a G-d who would allow it. Years later, though, one child would hear the story of his great-uncle, and it would affect him differently. He would find faith in the Creator and in his people. He would turn to Hashem whole-heartedly and devote his life to saving Jews. He left Spain to live among the religious *shtetls* of Eastern Europe. That boy is Abraham Lopez."

I was stunned and ashamed at the same time, and vowed to myself that, whatever might come, I would not lose my faith again.

Mama squeezed my hand and stood up. "Remember, Tzipporahla, everything works out for the best."

I would have dire need for that lesson in faith, for a few short days later my saintly father passed away. The day of his funeral was one of mingled sorrow and joy, for I was unable to attend, since I was delivering my first baby boy.

I had to remain in my cottage and was spared the sight of my mother sitting *shivah*, surrounded by ten of her children. The morning of my son's *bris*, my mother came to see me. I could tell that her emotions were waging war behind her weary eyes—the overwhelming battle between joyous pride and unfathomable grief, giving way to the stronger passions of despair and dejection.

She pressed her lips against the infant's warm head and rocked him back and forth rhythmically. "Oh, Tzipporahla. How can I ever go on? He was everything to me -- my strength, my courage, my faith. Without him I have nothing, I *am* nothing."

Agitated, I struggled to pull myself into a sitting position. "Mama, if ever there was a reason I was born, if ever I had one purpose in life, it would be to show you how wrong you are. It would be to give you back one-tenth of what you've given me all my life; to renew the faith and courage I know you have."

I was barely aware that I was crying, and I tugged earnestly at her sleeve. "Let me tell you a story that a wise and wonderful woman once told me as a child. Yes, Mama, I will never forget what I've learned at your knee.

"There once was a great king," I began slowly, carefully recounting the exact words that echoed distantly in my memory, "who imprisoned his physician. Bound in chains, the man spent many months fed only a small portion of barley bread and water each day.

"After a long time had passed, the king sent for the doctor to hear what the unhappy man had to say. To his surprise, the man was as hale and hearty as the day he had been imprisoned in his cell. When asked to what he owed his miraculous well being, the doctor answered that it was due to a brew of seven herbs he had prepared before he went to prison, and of which he drank a few drops every day. When asked what magic herbs they were, he responded, 'The first is absolute trust in the A-mighty, the second is hope, the third patience. The others are recognition of my sins, joy in the realization that in suffering now I will not have to suffer in the World to Come, relief in the thought that my punishment is not worse, and the knowledge that the same G-d who thrust me into this prison may free me at any moment.'"

Mama was nodding, her wet cheeks pressed against the reddened baby's face. "Do you hear that, little Chaim Hameln? Did you hear what your wise mama said? She will bring you up the way your blessed grandfather and I brought *her* up. Soon it will be Rosh Hashanah. It will signal the start of a new year and a new decade. You, my little one, will be the start of a new generation."

Watching Mama as she cradled Chaim Hameln Cleve in her arms, I thought I heard her say the words I knew she couldn't bring herself to utter at that moment. So I said them for her. "It's all for the best, Mama. This too is for the best."

EPILOGUE

The auction has neared its end and I remain lost in thought. My mind turns to another auction in the future, probably mine, and I wonder, what of value will be sold? Will this diary reach the auctioneer's hands? Will it be read by distant eyes of the future?

I shift the sleeping Chaim to my other arm. What world awaits him? What will the future bring him? Will the Mashiach come in his lifetime? In his children's?

The last item is brought to the block. My mother's fine lace tablecloth. She crocheted it herself as a girl. Countless times I sat at the table absently fingering the smooth white linen.

Gratefully I see Esther bidding for it. Mama's tablecloth shouldn't leave the family.

The auctioneer's hammer slams down. The sale is over, and so, it seems, is a huge part of Mama's life. She will begin again. It is all for the best.

I walk away from the auction empty-handed but not empty hearted. In my arms I hold the future, and inside I carry even more. From my father I have inherited a sense of justice as well as humor, and I have learned to adhere strictly to the law. From my mother I have gained a positive view of life, a strong belief in the A-mighty, and a love for family and traditions. These are my legacies. And these are what I hope to pass on to my children.